IF YOU WERE A TREE

Illustrated by: 1984-1985 1st Grade Class
Crestridge School, Omaha, Nebraska

Tell me now
If you were a tree
What kind of tree would you be?

Would you be thin and tall?
Round and small?
Narrow as a pin
Or wide as a wall?

Would you grow upside down
With your top in the ground
And roots in the sky
Like a bunch of worms trying to fly?

Tell me now.
Tell me about you as a tree.
What shape would you be?

Would you be like the letter ˜I˜?
Or round like an ˜O˜?
Or more divided like the letter ˜Y˜
˜Y˜ or ˜I˜ or ˜O˜,
Tell me now, tell me now.
Let me know!
How would you look?
How would you grow?

And as a tree
Where would you live?
By a snaky lake?
Or on an old dark twisty road
In the middle of an avenue?
Or on a 7th floor balcony with a view?

Maybe wedged in a cliff
On a mountain side
Or
Maybe, just maybe,

GEE!

Full and free
In a flower-filled valley?
Yes tell me now, tell me.
Where would you live if you were a tree?

And would other trees be near to you,
Just a branch shake away
For fun and play?

Or would you be
Far away from other trees—
Not near another tree at all
Where you would grow alone and tall.

And would you be funny?
Would you be a giggly tree?
TEE-HEE-HEE!
TEE-HEE-HEE!
Or would you be a quiet tree?
Not even whispering whispery sounds
To the silent ground all around?

Would you dance?
Dance with the breeze
And other trees
Sway free and gentle
As you please?

Wait! Wait!

Trees must eat.
Have some lunch.
Chomp some food.
Crunch, crunch, crunch, munch!

So as a tree
What would you eat
Besides sunlight at the stems
And water through your feet?

A licorice street
Or a fancy bed sheet?
Rhinoceros meat or
Gold winter wheat?
Warm, soft blueberry bread?
Or maybe even a spider head?
What would you eat if you were a tree?
Or would you just go hungry
Waiting for a treat of pickled,
Tickled, pink pig feet?

Would you welcome
Two and four-legged creatures
As your guests
And even "many" legged,
Some folks call "pest?"

What would be the homey things
You'd do best?
Would you nestle a house
Or house a nest
And be shade for those
Who want a cool rest?
Yes! Tell me, dear tree,
How you'd share your life with me.

And tell me, tell me.
You've got to do it!
Help me see what color tree you'd be.
Purple plum or peachy peach?
Apple red or cranberry cherry?
A rainbow tree with lots of dots?
Bright red circles like cinnamon hots?
Lime-lime green, banana yellow,
Apricot orange or Hawaiian punch Jell-O?
Or all the colors striped and squiggly
Moving in the wind, fishy wiggly?
I want to know, now tell me, tell me!
What color tree you would be?

And would there be bees and birds
And bears in your limbs?
And Christmas lights
With candy cane cones
And Christmas trims?

Would boys and girls hide in you?
And play a "scary" game of peek-a-boo?

Think of all the magic you could do,
Hiding the animals in the zoo.

And would you tell stories...MANY.
Or speak not any?
But think them just the same
And ask other trees to play
The Story Telling Tree guessing game?

Tell me now.
Tell me!
The magic I would see
If you could be your kind of tree.

And what would you, as a tree,
Make of yourself?
What would you be
After you've lived your life as a tree?
A polished desk?
A bedside chest?
A solid ball bat?
A door?
A ladder?
Or something like that?

Babby Ceratel

Wood for the fire?
A sailing boat?
Or maybe a canoe on the river afloat?
A toothpick?
A ladle?

Or maybe even a baby's cradle?

Yes! Yes!

I'm asking you
What, after a tree,
Would you be?

And as a tree,
Would you wonder why?

Why did I happen?
What made me be me?
I'm the only tree just like me.
Only I can be me.
Uniquely special, uniquely free!

Me! Me! Me!

The tree,
Growing deeper in the ground
And higher in the sky.
Celebrating life.
Celebrating earth.
Getting bigger and better
Every day since my birth.

ANIMAL INVENTIONS

Illustrated by: 1987-1988 2nd Grade Class
Conestoga School, Omaha, Nebraska

Match the Animals with the Inventions

 flying squirrel

 helicopter

 Spider

 hypodermic needle

 armadillo

 saw

 rabbit

backpack

 humming bird

 fishing net

 saw fish

 parachute

 Scorpion

 tank

 Kangaroo

 snowshoes

HI! My name is Tinker. I am an inventor. You can't see me because I live inside the brain of every boy and girl.

In some brains I sleep a lot; in others I'm always doing something. I love ideas and I love trying to make ideas into inventions.

Some of my ideas work very well; some fall apart or fail in other ways. One of my biggest failures was the boomerang bullet. I invented it to stop wars. I think it would have worked, except no one would test it.

Lots of my favorite inventions started because of my animal friends. Look at the previous page and see if you can tell which invention goes with which animal.

After you do that, I'll tell you how the animals helped me with these inventions. Just read through the book.

Five years ago I was in Canada making a big snowman. All of a sudden I fell through the snow. I was stuck there two hours.

Then a friendly white rabbit came along and dug me out with her powerful back legs. After that she gave me hot carrot soup to eat. Her name was Snows.

Snows said I could walk on the snow like she did if my feet were bigger.

I couldn't make my feet bigger but because of her idea I invented snowshoes. They worked!

When I saw Snows the next year she liked my creation.

We ran and played all day, skipping across the snow. After that, we had a big green salad. Lots of lettuce. Then Snows read me her favorite book, *Brer Rabbit*.

I was in Mexico drawing a picture of a cactus when my friend Stinger crawled by.

Stinger was a scorpion. He liked to lie in the hot sun and make up rhymes.

I told Stinger I liked rhymes so he read me one of his poems:

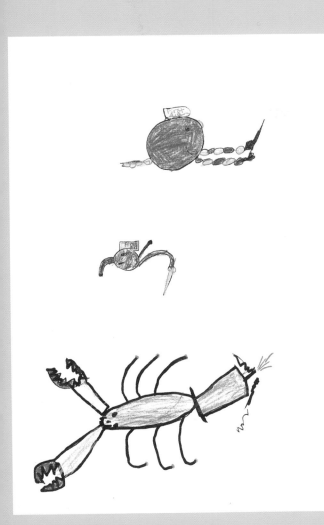

"My name is Stinger
I live where it's hot.
Safe...I am not.
With my needle-like tail,
Quick as a lick
I can make people sick.
By watching me you invented
The medicine-giving shot.
So the next time the doctor
Gives you the needle,
Thank the scorpion for what you got."

Then Stinger laughed and disappeared under a rock.

It was summer when I first saw Tiny the hummingbird. She was floating among the wildflowers in the park. I watched her non-stop for fifteen minutes.

I couldn't believe my eyes! Tiny went up, down, sideways, and even backwards. Her wings were going so fast you couldn't see them.

I said hello. Tiny hummed hello back. We were friends from the start and played all afternoon.

The next summer I came back in a machine that worked like Tiny.

"Where did you get that funny looking thing?" she asked.

"I invented it by watching you," I replied.

"You're kidding!" Tiny chuckled. "It looks like an eggbeater."

Well, some people call it that. I named it Helicopter! Tiny laughed then got in and took a ride with me.

I would have never met Floater or invented the parachute if I didn't love to climb trees.

It was almost dark and I was deep in an African forest. I had just climbed thirty feet up a tree hunting wild fruit when I saw a squirrel fly from one tree to another 250 feet away. "Wow. What a trick!" I yelled.

Floater heard me and floated right to where I was. "No trick," he said. "I'm made to do that; see I have extra skin between my legs and body."

I imagined being able to fly like Floater. It was in a dream two years later when I thought up the parachute.

Floater wondered why I put all those colors and designs on it. He said I was nutty. Since squirrels like nuts, I thought that was okay.

I first met Spidey while pulling weeds in my garden. (My garden has lots of weeds.)

Spidey is a spider and she was making a web. She told me it was her house. I liked how it was shiny in the orange sun.

Spidey would catch flies and moths and other insects in her web. She said she loved insects...for lunch, dinner, and snacks.

Spidey taught me how to make webs too. I called them nets. Now I can catch things.

One day when we were talking, Spidey told me her favorite nursery rhyme was "Little Miss Muffet".

Tuff the turtle doesn't talk much. He is shy and quiet.

One cool, rainy April morning when he didn't know I was near, I heard Tuff whisper to his friend, Hank the armadillo, "People have us to thank for the tank."

Hank said, "Yes!"

Colors the chameleon, who was lying next to Hank but couldn't be seen, said, "That's right, Tinker. The inventor made the tank by watching both of you." I just kept quiet and smiled.

Tuff put his head back into his shell. He probably went back to licking his slowpoke sucker, which he's had since Valentine's Day, 1980.

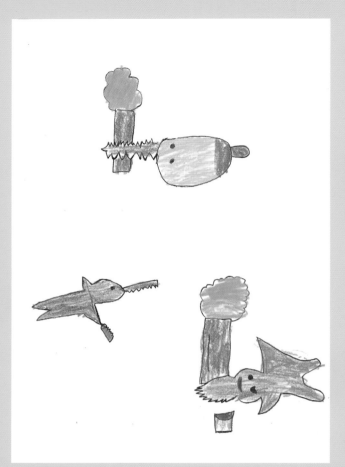

I met Cutter while swimming in the Atlantic Ocean last September. I was on vacation in Key West, Florida, with my mom and dad.

Cutter is a sawfish. His long nose has 32 little, cutting blades on it. As he swam around he used his saw-like nose to dig for food in mulch and sand on the ocean floor.

It worked well. When I got home I thought about Cutter. After a while I invented the knife and saw for cutting things.

I sent Cutter a drawing of what I had made. He sent it back all sliced up in 32 pieces. That meant he liked the invention!

Cutter doesn't like the nets Spidey taught me to make.

When I was seven years old I went on a long hike in Australia. The hike was lots of fun but I kept dropping my compass, tent, and sack of food.

I had just dropped my tent for the third time when...*plop*! A kangaroo hopped next to me and said, "Hi, my name is Jumpsy. It looks like you need a pouch like I have to carry your things." Then Jumpsy bounced away.

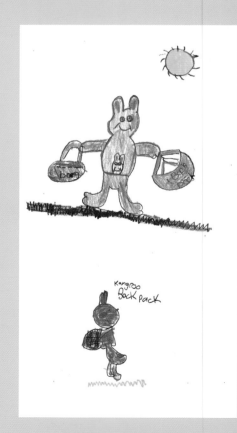

Kangaroo Back pack

When I got home I remembered Jumpsy's pouch and made my own kind of pouch. I called it a backpack. I was proud of my backpack.

The next year I returned to Australia with my backpack. I was able to hike lots further and carry more. I found Jumpsy and gave her some berries. Kangaroos love berries; red and blue ones. I was able to carry them in my backpack.

I have lots more animal friends who helped me think up other inventions.

Watch animals real close: how they move, how they look, and what they do. Maybe you will even come up with your own brand new invention.

Think about all the animals. Then get a piece of paper and draw them with the inventions.

I hope you do! Inventing can be lots of fun!

Your friend, Tinker

Match the Animals with the Inventions

flying squirrel — helicopter

spider — hypodermic needle

armadillo — saw

rabbit — backpack

humming bird — fishing net

saw fish — parachute

scorpion — tank

kangaroo — snowshoes

MOTHER EARTH AND HER STAR FRIENDS

Illustrated by: 1989-1990 1st Grade Class
Room 5 Crestridge School, Omaha, Nebraska

Once in a time, four young stars from deep, dark space travelled above the little blue, brown, and green planet called Earth. This place in the sky was their new home.

Two of the stars were boys, named Etat and Mada, and two of the stars were girls. Their names were Nosilla and Enna. The whole sky was their playground and they moved across it freely like clouds cross over land. They were very bright stars and full of good energy.

Earth would change from light to dark, day to night.
The young stars learned that Earth's father, the Sun, made
this happen. With the change from light to dark, they played
hide-and-go-seek in the sky in the Sun's rays. The Sun's rays
were so bright no one could see or find them.

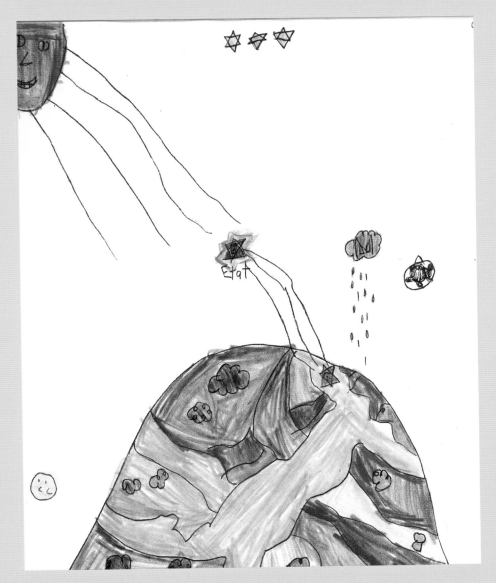

Etat loved Earth most for her clean, fresh waters; all the oceans, lakes, rivers, and ponds. And the storm clouds that brought Earth the rain and snow which helped make these big waters.

Etat could see himself sparkle in the waters and he smiled when he did. He was especially happy when he saw himself reflecting on the ocean because his light spread so far, and he looked so big, and the ocean waves made his reflection dance.

Enna loved Earth too! She really liked the very warm and very cold parts of this tiny planet. The cold air parts seemed to make Enna sparkle and shine brighter. When this happened, many more stars could be seen. This gave Enna more friends. The warm air parts made Enna feel soft and look like she was wearing a rosy red gown all around her.

Mada loved Earth's creatures: birds, fish, insects, mammals, and even the two-legged creatures called humans. Mada would watch these creatures for days and days without blinking or even sleeping. He often laughed and giggled at the funny way many of these creatures moved, like kangaroos hopping and pelicans diving into the sea.

Nosilla also loved Earth. She loved everything that grew from the ground: trees, plants, flowers, grass, and even weeds. She just thought of weeds as another kind of flower. Nosilla loved how there were so many different kinds with many different shapes and colors.

Nosilla was very smart and knew the water that Etat liked and the light from Father Sun were the food that kept these growing things alive. Nosilla also knew that the trees, plants, flowers, and weeds were homes for many of the creatures Mada enjoyed watching.

Yes, Nosilla, Etat, Enna, and Mada all had their special reasons for loving this beautiful, tiny planet, Earth.

But they all shared another reason even more special. They discovered that Earth was not a dead rock in space but an alive, loving, healthy, body all by itself. Etat, Nosilla, Mada, and Enna marveled at how naturally Earth shared her love, aliveness, and health with everything else which lived upon her. Like a mother, Earth worked hard to make all upon her one large and healthy family.

   As the four young stars talked to Earth in their own way with twinkles and bright glows, Earth made them feel like welcomed guests. Earth seemed to always be giving.

   Nosilla, Etat, Mada, and Enna all knew Earth had a big heart. In fact, one day Nosilla said, "You know, I discovered that if you move the letter `H´ in the word Earth and put it before the letter `E´, it spells Heart. You know, I think Earth was named Heart once in a time."

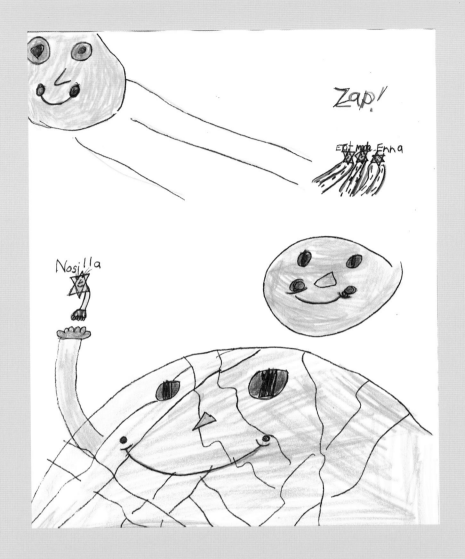

Etat, Enna, and Mada twinkled with happiness and delight at the wisdom of their sister star. When they did, extra beams of light flashed from them. *Zap!* The night sky looked like early morning. Earth smiled to them and they each knew Earth was their friend with a healthy, loving heart.

Nosilla, Mada, Enna, and Etat had a scare one day. They saw that some of the two-legged creatures (called humans) had pictures of Earth looking all broken into pieces. Mada learned these pictures were called world maps.

At first they thought Earth had maybe fallen and was cracked like a colored Easter egg. But from high up they could see that Earth was not broken.

Mada found out these maps were just the way most of the two-legged creatures decided things, like where to live and how to find their way around.

Earth didn't like the way these maps made her look all cracked and broken but she was patient with the young human creatures. She knew that when their kind grew older like the birds, fish, and mammals, the maps wouldn't be needed anymore and would be thrown away. The humans would feel and be more free on Mother Earth. This idea gave Earth much happiness.

This time with the four young stars was very special and good for Earth. She now felt healthier and more alive. Nosilla, Etat, Mada, and Enna gave Earth new hope. Every day, more and more of Earth's family would look to and learn from these wise stars. More and more good deeds got done and Earth's family was more caring.

Every April, the humans celebrated a special day all over the tiny planet Earth. They called it Earth Day. And each year, Earth's heart beat stronger and louder because of it.

Nosilla, Etat, Mada, and Enna had great fun enjoying Earth Day. They were especially happy about the day because the water, air, growing things, and creatures, which they loved so much, were being talked about and cared for by the humans.

    As days passed, Nosilla, Mada, Etat, and Enna continued to sparkle, glow, and play in the sky.

    ...Some of Earth's family wondered if more stars like Nosilla, Mada, Etat, and Enna would move in above them.

    ...Others were sure there would be more.

    ...Some dreamed of being young stars themselves.

    ...And some were already acting like stars.

The story behind these three children's book
By Jim Meier

In the 1980s, I wrote three children's stories with the intent to make them books. They needed to be illustrated and colored. I wanted this 'work' to be done by young children. My wife Cindy and I had three children, sons, Tate and Adam, and daughter, Allison. So resources were at the ready. Their Omaha Public School classmates provided more creative, uninhibited artists. With much assistance from my children's teachers, Astride Winslade for books 1 and 3, and Denise Vanzago for book 2, each story now had 20-25 eager, imaginative, pencil-ready artists to give the stories images.

The three books are:

Book Title	# of Drawings	My Child	Grade	Year	School
If You Were A Tree	18	Son, Tate	1st	'84-'85	Crestridge Elementary, Omaha, NE
Nature's Inventions	9	Son, Adam	2nd	'87-'88	Conestoga Elementary, Omaha, NE
Mother Earth and Her Star Friends	14	Daughter, Allison	1st	'89-'90	Crestridge Elementary, Omaha, NE

I've been asked why, why create this way? Simple:

1. I wanted to be involved with my kids in their classroom early; before it just wouldn't be cool showing up.
2. Since I coach and train adults how to become more creative and innovative in their work, I wanted to test some of those tools and techniques with kids.
3. To demonstrate the children's motivation to draw was intrinsic. The process itself was the reward and recognition. (There was no mention of candy, cake, trinkets, etc. or any given during the process.)
4. To increase the self-esteem of the children.
5. To give the story visual life which would help teach the story content*.
6. To partner with kids in producing a product that would teach other kids and adults.
7. My ability to draw is weak.
8. To play at a higher level.

Also, among my professional specialties as a trainer, consultant, and coach is teaching individuals, work teams and entire organizations 18 characteristics of the creative mind, and the process for developing and unleashing those characteristics. Thus, creating and completing these three children's books became a way for me to apply what I teach.

*Key points about the content of each book:

A)   The pictures drawn by the child in **If You Were a Tree** provide insight to that child's personality. I am certified in the administration, interpretation, and use of the widely used personality inventory, the Myers-Briggs Type Indicator (MBTI). Many of the questions in this book's story help a teacher and parent better understand the child from this personality prism. However, a caution: Any version of the Myers-Briggs Type Indicator, let alone a children's book, should not be used to draw distinct conclusions about a child's personality. At 6 and 7 years of age, it is too early to do so.

B)   Both the words and pictures in **Animal Inventions** help pique curiosity and expand knowledge in the child and hopefully the adults reading it too. Additionally, it demonstrates the value of observation skills and linking those observations to other worlds of knowledge. Plus, this book is intended to reveal the richness of life lessons among the many creatures that inhabit planet Earth.

C)   The story, **Mother Earth and Her Star Friends**, is abstract even for adults, let alone for a younger, developing mind. The fact that these first graders could draw easy-to-interpret images about the story is testimony to their cognitive development. This story required these young children to play with the awesome bigness of our universe. By giving Earth and the four stars human qualities, the book creates a connectedness to the reality that Earth is not a dead rock but a complex, living, and changing organism; an organism we humans must help steward and can learn from if only we listen. The drawings wonderfully reflect this theme.

The step-by-step process used with all three books:

1.   I wrote the story.
2.   I read the story to the class.
3.   The teacher and I decided where to 'carve up' the story text into segments to be illustrated.
4.   The teacher read the each segment and the kids drew a picture to go along with the words. The teacher and I agreed ahead of time she would not influence or guide them in any way other than explain the meaning of a word in case a student(s) didn't understand it. She simply said something like, "Do you remember the story Mr. Meier read to you? Guess what! You get to draw pictures about the story so we can make it into a book." Over several months the class drew one picture per segment. No more than two segments per week. They put their names on the back.
5.   From the 20-25 drawings per segment, I selected the one I thought best matched the story's words using three criteria: imagination, clarity, and originality. Many drawings matched these criteria.

6. After making my selection, I looked at the name on the back. After realizing one or more children had 2-3 drawings picked, I applied a fourth criterion, no more than one drawing from one child. I wanted to include the work of as many children as possible.
7. Some of the curves, twists, lines, and shapes in the drawings needed to be darker. I darkened them. No other changes were made to any of the images. (With the 2nd and 3rd books, the kids were told to press harder with their pencils. They did and those two books had very few parts of a drawing darkened.)
8. I made 25-30 photo copies of each chosen drawing.
9. The photo copies, along with two boxes of 60 colored pencils, were given to the teacher.
10. Over the course of several months, one by one, the photo copied drawings were given to the class along with the colored pencils to share. Now originality, youthful unconscious minds, and productive playfulness took added form. The same black and white images were taken for a spin on the color wheel. As you would expect, after going down this track, no two colored images came back with the same rich array of colors. Some made 'the finish line' having stayed within the lines. And of course, there were those colored pictures where the 'nonconforming' child 'drove' his/her colored pencils outside the lines. No tickets were issued!
11. Once all pictures were colored by every student, I choose the 'best' five for each drawing and assembled them into a bound book. I did not know which student colored which drawing. The five bound books included the title, each student's name, their teacher's name, school, grade, date, and my name on a cover page. Each of the three books that are reproduced in this volume is one of those original five. None of the colored pictures were altered in any way.
12. A copy of one of the originals of each of the three books was placed in the school library.
13. Two of the originals of each of the three books were given as a gift to business, government, and community leaders in Nebraska and Omaha*. At these celebrations several of the children read passages from their book.

   ***If You Were A Tree** Harold Anderson, then President of the *Omaha World-Herald* newspaper and Eugene Mahoney, then Director of the Nebraska Game and Parks Commission

   ***Nature's Inventions** Dr. Lee Simmons, Executive Director, Henry Doorly Zoo and senior executive from the Omaha Zoological Society

   ***Mother Earth and Her Star Friends** P.J. Morgan, then mayor of Omaha and 3 representations of The Earth Day in Omaha project, 1990

14. The school was also given an uncolored copy for the library.
15. Each child from the class was given an uncolored copy of the book, the book was read again by class members, and all enjoyed juice and piece of cake. This was a surprise and as mentioned earlier, not a stated reward upfront or during the process.

Jim Meier is a globally-recognized author, speaker, consultant, leadership and sports psychology coach, advisor, and radio show host. Since 1976 he has assisted people in unleashing their inner gifts and becoming a better version of their present self. His customers are from many organization sectors: business, education, government, sports, healthcare, the military, non-profits, and professional and civic associations.

Contact information:
Cell: 402-490-9293
e-mail: meier260@cox.net
web address: www.championshipthinkingcoach.com

Adam Meier, 1987 - dreaming up more animal inspired inventions with family dog, Sneakers, helping

Allison Meier reading to Mayor P J Morgan Mother Earth and her Star Friends

Allison Meier, Earth Day 1990 - pointing to her drawing in *Mother Earth and Her Star Friends*

Adam Meier tinkering and building with legos